DISNEY

CLUB PENGUIN

Secret Agent Handbook

By Katherine Noll
Grosset & Dunlap

GROSSET & DUNLAP
Published by the Penguin Group
Penguin Group (USA) Inc., 375 Hudson Street, New York, New York 10014, USA
Penguin Group (Canada), 90 Eglinton Avenue East, Suite 700,
Toronto, Ontario M4P 2Y3, Canada
(a division of Pearson Penguin Canada Inc.)
Penguin Books Ltd., 80 Strand, London WC2R 0RL, England
Penguin Group Ireland, 25 St. Stephen's Green, Dublin 2, Ireland
(a division of Penguin Books Ltd.)
Penguin Group (Australia), 250 Camberwell Road,
Camberwell, Victoria 3124, Australia
(a division of Pearson Australia Group Pty. Ltd.)
Penguin Books India Pvt. Ltd., 11 Community Centre,
Panchsheel Park, New Delhi–110 017, India
Penguin Group (NZ), 67 Apollo Drive, Rosedale,
North Shore 0632, New Zealand (a division of Pearson New Zealand Ltd.)
Penguin Books (South Africa) (Pty.) Ltd., 24 Sturdee Avenue,
Rosebank, Johannesburg 2196, South Africa

Penguin Books Ltd., Registered Offices:
80 Strand, London WC2R 0RL, England

Library of Congress Control Number: 2008047687

ISBN 978-0-448-45096-4   10 9 8 7 6 5 4

Penguin Secret Agency

Dear Penguins,

We are the Penguin Secret Agency (PSA), an organization created to keep Club Penguin safe. The PSA relies on a group of special penguins to be our eyes and ears. They are called secret agents.

The penguin sledding down the Ski Hill next to you could be a secret agent. So could the penguin drilling on the Iceberg. You yourself might be a secret agent. But the word to remember is *secret*. Secret agents never reveal their identities. They work undercover. You'll never know if a secret agent is around.

This book contains highly confidential information. Inside you'll discover everything you need to know about being an agent and the answers to some of Club Penguin's biggest mysteries. We'll also test your powers of observation and problem-solving abilities to help you be the most resourceful agent around.

Our motto is "Be Resourceful, Be Remarkable, Be Ready." If you think you possess these qualities, keep reading to discover how you can join the PSA today. If you're already a secret agent, you can skip ahead to page 9.

Good luck,

o

Becoming a Secret Agent

If you're not already a member of the PSA, do you have what it takes to become one? Apply by clicking the  icon and then click on "Become a Secret Agent." You have to be at least 30 days old. Follow the instructions and your application will be submitted. Experienced agents, including the Director of the PSA, will review your application.

Always on Duty

Becoming a secret agent is a privilege, but it comes with responsibility. Whether you are having fun at a party or hanging out at the Pizza Parlor, a secret agent must always report to the moderator any signs of trouble. Here are some things an agent needs to be on the lookout for:

- Penguins using bad language
- Penguins giving out their real name, location, or phone numbers, or asking other penguins for that information
- Penguins being mean or rude to other penguins
- Penguins asking for passwords

An agent must immediately report these types of behavior. It doesn't matter if you were about to try and break your high score on *Astro-Barrier* or if you were heading over to the Gift Shop to check out the latest fashions. Your duty as an agent must always come first.

Agents are also encouraged to help other penguins. Perhaps a new penguin is waddling around, looking lost. Offer to give him or her a tour of the island. Maybe a penguin is looking for the latest pin, or wondering how to catch the mullet in *Ice Fishing*. If you know the answer, share it.

Put to the Test

As part of the application, you will have to take a quiz. You must answer every question correctly or your application won't be reviewed. You can take the quiz as many times as you want.

If the PSA decides you are ready to hit the field, they'll send you a spy phone. It will show up on your screen, the next time you log in to Club Penguin.

Agents need many skills. But to begin with, agents have to know a lot about Club Penguin. Take this test to see if you've got the know-how to be an agent.

1. What does it mean if a penguin is wearing a hat with a "?" on it?
   a. The penguin wants to ask you a question.
   b. The penguin submitted a riddle to *The Club Penguin Times*.
   c. The penguin is a Tour Guide.

2. Penguins should be reported to the moderator for saying what type of personal information?
   a. Whether they are a boy or a girl
   b. Their address
   c. Their favorite ice cream flavor

3. What item is always hidden in the Penguin Style catalog?
   a. The silver surfboard
   b. The red Viking Helmet
   c. The pink swim goggles

4. Which is a reason to report a penguin to the moderator?
   a. Being mean or rude
   b. Throwing snowballs
   c. Not saying hello to you

5. Where does the manhole cover in the Plaza lead to?
   a. The Lighthouse
   b. The Underground Pool
   c. The Night Club

6. Pick one quality that you think a secret agent should have.
   a. Bossy
   b. Honest
   c. Tough

7. Where should you go if you want to play *Jet Pack Adventure*?
   a. The Dock
   b. Ski Hill
   c. The Beacon

8. Which puffle did Rockhopper bring to Club Penguin from Rockhopper Island?
   a. The blue puffle
   b. The pink puffle
   c. The red puffle

9. What is the name of the yellow bird in the cuckoo clock at the Ski Lodge?
   a. Missy
   b. Fluffy
   c. Fred

10. What is a good reason to become a secret agent?
    a. To get the supercool spy phone
    b. To keep Club Penguin safe
    c. So you can brag to all of your friends

PSA Challenge
TEST YOURSELF: ANSWERS

Give yourself 1 point for each correct answer.

1. C; 2. B; 3. B; 4. A; 5. B; 6. B; 7. C; 8. C; 9. C; 10. B

If you scored 9-10 points:
Congratulations! You are sure to be a credit to the PSA. We are looking for penguins exactly like you.

If you scored 7-8 points:
Good work! You might have been stumped by a couple of the harder questions, but you have got what it takes to be a good agent.

If you scored 6 or fewer points:
Getting the skills to become a superior secret agent is not easy, so don't despair! Try exploring Club Penguin more. If you're not sure about something, ask other penguins. Before you know it, you'll be acing this quiz and tackling secret agent missions.

Apply Today!
If you think you've got the skills to be a secret agent, apply now. The rest of the information in this handbook is top secret.

WARNING

Everything beyond this page is highly confidential and for secret agents' eyes ONLY.

RESTRICTED AREA

AUTHORIZED PERSONNEL ONLY

NO PEEKING

THIS MEANS YOU!

☐☐⌧L⌧⌧☐ ☐☐L⌧☐☐ ⌐⌐☐⌧☐. ⌧⌧⌧L☐☐☐.

Greetings, agent! Most penguins know me as Gary the Gadget Guy, Club Penguin's resident inventor. But savvy agents like you know me as G. I work behind the scenes to help keep Club Penguin safe, just like you. But my main job at the Penguin Secret Agency is to make gadgets you can use when you're out in the field. I also notify agents whenever a situation requires their attention and explain assignments. But, of course, you already know this from the missions we've worked on together.

Like you, I've also been privy to a lot of classified information as an agent, including receiving orders directly from the leader of the PSA. Many have asked me about the identity of this mysterious penguin, but like all agents the director prefers to keep his or her identity a secret.

Penguin Puzzles

When you see a PENGUIN PUZZLE, put your thinking cap on. I will test your problem-solving skills with a puzzle or a riddle. You'll need the secret code on the inside front cover of this book to decipher the answers. I might even slip some jokes into this section. I may be a hard-working scientist, but I've got a sense of humor, too.

Fast Facts

I firmly believe that a good scientist never stops learning. One of the ways that I exercise my brain is by reading. I have stacks of books and scientific journals in my workshop, and whenever I have some free time I enjoy perusing them. I've discovered some fascinating facts doing this. Throughout this handbook, I'll be sharing some of my favorite ones with you. Secret agents know that knowledge is power. A little bit of information can be just the thing needed to crack a tough mission.

PENGUIN PUZZLE

If you have it, you want to share it, but if you share it, you don't have it. What is it? ⌐ ⌐◻⌐⌐☒◻⌐

One of the most important skills an agent can have is to be observant. Study this picture carefully for a few minutes, then turn the page and see how many questions you can answer about this scene.

Now let's see how much you can remember.
No peeking!

1. What is the black puffle in the cage doing?

   _____

   ◌▯x ☐☐ x⌐ x⌐

2. What does the door underneath the Exit sign say on it?

   _____

   ☐x xx x ◌☐☐ ◌

3. What is the blue penguin holding?

   _____

   ⌐ ◌☐xx x◌ x◌⌐⌐x☐

4. How many puffles are in the pen?

   _____

   ⌐⌐◌☐

5. What is the red puffle eating?

   _____

   ⌐ ⌐xxx⌐☐

6. What color is the fish inside the fishbowl?

_____

⊠ ⊠ ⌋⊠ ⌐ □

7. What color is the puffle standing on top of the bags of puffle food?

_____

⊓ □ ⊠ ⊠ ⊠ ⊙

8. What color puffle was in the large puffle bed?

_____

⌐ ⊠ □ □ ⊠

Welcome to HQ

When you enter Headquarters, or HQ, you'll see a wall of twenty-four state-of-the-art monitors that show almost every room on Club Penguin. If trouble is spotted, agents will be dispatched right away. Agents can get to HQ two ways: by teleporting with their spy phones, or by going through a secret entrance in the Sport Shop. (It's the dressing room closest to the shop's front door.)

The PSA was created in 2006. Its mission was and still is to keep Club Penguin a safe place. But soon the director decided the agency needed to be expanded. The PSA spared no expense as it built the current Headquarters.

The PSA also added the Gadget Room, where G invents the gadgets that agents use on missions. You can often find G here working late and drinking lots of coffee.

FAST FACT

A single snowstorm can produce 40 million tons of snow. According to my computations, that would make approximately 160 million snow penguins.

PENGUIN PUZZLE

The more of them you take, the more you leave behind. What are they? □☒☒◻◻◻◻☒◻

PSA Challenge
SECRET AGENT SCAVENGER HUNT

All agents must know how to quickly get from one place to another on the island. Put your skills to the test with this scavenger hunt. Club Penguin is different each time you log in. Penguins are always up to something new. But here's a list of some common sights you may often see on the island. Use your spy phone to teleport around the island quickly. See how many things you can find on the list below and check them off as you go. You can also get some secret agent friends together and do this as a group activity.

- ☐ A penguin giving a tour
- ☐ Penguins throwing snowballs
- ☐ A penguin dancing
- ☐ Penguins swimming
- ☐ The latest pin
- ☐ A penguin looking through binoculars or a telescope
- ☐ A penguin walking a puffle
- ☐ Penguins acting on The Stage
- ☐ A hidden item in the Penguin Style catalog
- ☐ Penguins playing *Find Four*
- ☐ Penguins sitting on a couch
- ☐ A penguin tossing pizza dough
- ☐ A penguin working as a waiter
- ☐ A hidden item in the Snow and Sports catalog
- ☐ Penguins playing ice hockey
- ☐ A penguin playing a musical instrument
- ☐ Penguins sitting by a fire
- ☐ Penguins playing *mancala*
- ☐ A penguin pouring coffee
- ☐ A penguin sitting in a sled
- ☐ A penguin reading *The Club Penguin Times*

Spy Gear

The right tools can really help on a mission. A good agent knows that creative thinking and hard work can solve even the toughest missions. But sometimes an agent may come across an obstacle that seems impossible to overcome. That's where the gadgets I make come in. If there is a need for something, I immediately go to work to find a solution. Throughout this section, I'm going to share with you some of the inventions that I have created for the PSA. A lot of scientific research has gone into these high-tech gadgets.

The Spy Phone

The first thing you receive when you become an agent is the model #102405 Spy Phone. You teleport at the touch of a button and the phone is equipped with useful tools. Try using the phone's wrench, comb, and scissors when you encounter something that needs to be fixed. You never know what might work.

PENGUIN PUZZLE

You answer me even though I never ask you any questions. What am I? ⅃ ⓐⓞⓧⓟⓧⓝⓧⓧⓞ

LONG-RANGE ANTENNA
Allows you to keep in contact with HQ no matter where you are on Club Penguin.

LED BLINKING LIGHT
Click on this light to access your spy tools.

VIEW SCREEN
Shows the names of different rooms. Click on the screen to change the room names or use the teleporter scroll button.

AGENT HQ

Teleport

Visit HQ

TELEPORT
Click to teleport to room showing on view screen.

TELEPORTER SCROLL BUTTON
Click to scroll between room names.

14.3 hz AUDITORY IMPULSE RECEPTOR
State-of-the-art technology makes sure your reception is crystal clear.

VISIT HQ
Push this button and you'll instantly be teleported to HQ.

The Gadget Room

Many a time you can find me in the Gadget Room, working late and poring over the blueprints of my latest invention. You'll also find many of my creations, including test models, in the Gadget Room.

The Gadget Room is one of the most secure places on the entire island, with even more security precautions in place than HQ. This is because of all of the equipment found here. If these creations were to fall into the wrong hands, particularly the furry white paws of a certain polar bear, the consequences would be dire! (To learn more about one of the PSA's biggest threats, Herbert P. Bear, turn to page 40.)

The thick steel doors are monitored by multiple security cameras. I alone can open the doors by using the eye scanner, a special piece of machinery that responds to my eyes only. When you are working on a mission and need access to the Gadget Room, I will grant you special access.

Whenever you are granted access to this room, make sure to take a good look around. Even if an item can't help on your current mission, it may come in handy at a later date. Don't be afraid to touch some of the equipment and try it out. You'll find that the boom box packs a ton of sound, and my alarm clock is extra loud, too.

FAST FACT

Even a diligent scientist such as myself needs to relax now and then. When I'm looking for some quiet time, I grab my fishing pole and do a bit of ice fishing. But it seems my brain is always at work, and I couldn't help but notice: The fish I caught didn't have any ears. So how do they hear? Fish do not have ears on the outside of their bodies. Instead, they have internal ears located inside their bodies, which they use to hear sound vibrations in the water.

MISSION HELPERS

Many cases are solved when a clever agent combines everyday items to solve the problem at hand. But if you are stuck, come and talk to me. I might have just the invention to help you out.

AC 1000 Fan Prototype

Fans can be more than cooling systems for an igloo. Sometimes a portable breeze is just what you need to blow a clue your way. Look for your chance to use this item in Mission ⬚ ⌐◙⬚.

Crab Translator 3000

How do you interview a witness who happens to be a crab? With the Crab Translator 3000, of course! I'm still working out a few glitches in this invention. See what happens when I try to use it in Mission ◙⌐◙.

Fedora Propeller Hat

Penguins fly using the jet pack, but some puffles are known to float around wearing a propeller hat. If you are trying to get an item that's just out of reach, perhaps a friendly puffle will grab it for you if you provide them with this hat. See what happens in Mission □□□□□.

Furensic Analyzer 3000

If you find a tuft of fur that has got you puzzled, head over to the Gadget Room and I'll place it in the Furensic Analyzer 3000. This gizmo will tell us which creature the fur is from and also identify any foreign objects that might be on it. This machine will come in handy during Mission □ □□□.

Electromagnet 1000

If you need to grab something large and heavy that is made of metal, an ordinary magnet won't do. This ultra-strong one can do the trick, especially in Mission □□□□□.

POWA BOX

Life Preserver Shooter

Take aim and fire with this handy shooter. It launches life preservers to penguins in distress, whether they are stranded on an iceberg or a mountainside. You'll find this invention particularly helpful in Mission ☒☒☐ and Mission ☐☒◩☒.

Night Vision Goggles

You might have to chase down clues or solve a problem in the darkest of places. That's where these goggles come in handy. You'll find them especially useful in Mission ◩⊓☒☐☐.

Super Helium

Need a lift? If you come across some balloons during Mission ☐⌐⌐⊓◩, you should ask me about this item. It might raise your case to new heights!

Tracking Goggles

Sometimes you'll need to spy clues that can't be seen by the ordinary eye.

You'll be surprised what these tracking goggles will help you discover in Mission ☐⌐⌐◙☐.

Test Chamber

You can't take this machine out into the field with you. You'll have to use it in the Gadget Room. Stuck? Try bringing items you aren't sure how to use to the Gadget Room and placing them one at a time in the Test Chamber. A little heat or frost could help you crack your case. You can't complete Mission ◙☐◙☐☒ without this invention.

TEST CHAMBER

PSA Challenge
BLUEPRINT BLAST OFF

A successful agent must learn how to combine everyday items to create something new. Here are blueprints I created for a simple rocket. Get to work and see if you can make it blast off.

You will need:

- An uninflated balloon
- A long piece of string, about 12 feet long
- A clothespin
- A plastic drinking straw, the kind that does not bend
- Tape

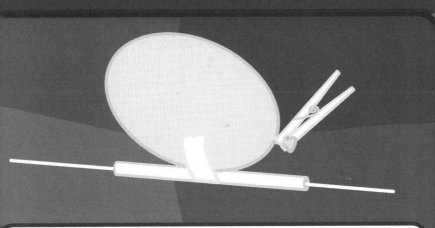

1. Blow up the balloon but do not tie it shut.
2. Attach the clothespin to the open end of the balloon.
3. Tape the balloon to the straw lengthwise so that the opening of the balloon is facing you.
4. Tie one end of the string onto a doorknob.
5. Thread the string through the drinking straw.
6. Pull the string tight and secure it by tying it onto a chair or any other object.
7. Slide the straw down the string so it's closest to you.
8. Release the clothespin and launch your rocket!

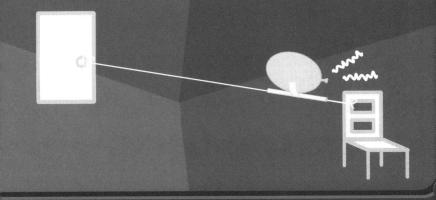

The F.I.S.H.

F.I.S.H. stands for the Factual Informative Spy Handbook—a book that has got everything you need to know about being a secret agent in it.

It also includes Club Penguin secrets and super spy clothes that you can buy if you have a membership to Club Penguin. You can find it in HQ in the lower right-hand corner of the screen.

THE F.I.S.H.

(FACTUAL INFORMATIVE SPY HANDBOOK)

FAST FACT

The largest snowflake on record was 15 inches wide and 8 inches thick. That's about the size of a Pizzatron 3000's Supreme Sizzle Pizza with extra toppings.

PENGUIN PUZZLE

A secret agent put ten pounds of spy gear into a bag. He put one more thing in the bag and now it weighs less. What was it? ⅃ ⊓⊠⋉□

Dress the Part

Even though being an agent is a secret, you can still dress the part. In the F.I.S.H, you can buy special spy clothes. The clothing items change, so keep checking back to see what's new.

As you travel around the island, you might notice other penguins dressed the same way. They're not necessarily agents. The clothing items sold in the F.I.S.H. are also available from time to time in the Penguin Style catalog. So you don't have to worry about blowing your cover by wearing them.

PSA Challenge
MASTER OF DISGUISE

Sometimes an agent needs to go undercover. For each scenario, pick one clothing item from each row below to make a disguise. Then write the letters in the spaces provided.

ROW 1	ROW 2	ROW 3

a. Cowboy hat   a. Admiral's jacket   a. Cowboy boots

b. Safari hat   b. Green shorts   b. Stardust Slippers

c. Straw hat   c. Dazzle dress   c. Lasso

d. Tricorn hat   d. Cowboy vest   d. Parrot

e. Supreme Diva wig   e. Beige explorer outfit   e. Surfboard

1. The show must go on! The power went out at the Lighthouse—right as a country music band was playing on the stage. Your job is to get the lights back on and keep the concert going.

   Row 1: _____   Row 2: _____   Row 3: _____

   Answer: Row 1: ⌟; Row 2: ⌍; Row 3: ⌟

2. Surf's up! G has sent you to investigate a possible sighting of a large white bear at the Surf Hut.

   Row 1: _____   Row 2: _____   Row 3: _____

   Answer: Row 1: ∟; Row 2: ⊔; Row 3: □

3. Something strange has been spotted at the opening night of The Quest for the Golden Puffle—and it's not just the crocodiles that are part of the set! Someone claims to have seen some bear prints in the snow. You need to get to The Stage, and fast.

   Row 1: _____   Row 2: _____   Row 3: _____

   Answer: Row 1: ⊔; Row 2: □; Row 3: ∟

4. Rockhopper's in town and he needs your help. He can't find his trusty sidekick, Yarr. Head over to the Beach and start looking.

   Row 1: _____   Row 2: _____   Row 3: _____

   Answer: Row 1: ⌍; Row 2: ⌟; Row 3: ⌍

The Secret Code

Sometimes the PSA needs to send its agents a secret message. But what if the message were to fall into the wrong hands? The director decided that a secret code needed to be developed. The code would allow the PSA to send messages to its agents without anyone else being able to read them. G went to work and the code was created. In fact, the code has been used throughout this book. You can see a chart of the code on the inside cover of the front of this book.

It's called the Tic-Tac-Toe code. That's because it's based on the tic-tac-toe game. It's easy to remember. For the letters from *A* to *I*, the grid is blank. For *J* to *R*, just put an *X* in the spaces, and for *S* to *Z*, put an *O* in them.

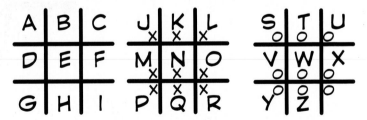

Don't worry if you can't remember it right away. When you are on a mission, the code is always available on the bottom right-hand corner of your screen.

PSA Challenge

SOLVE THE SECRET MESSAGE

The Director of the PSA has sent you an important message. Use the secret code to decipher it. Then turn to the next page and see how many questions you can answer about the case.

Find the ⊠□⊠⊐�****⊏⊏⊠ wearing the ⊠□⊐ ⊔⊔�◺□◺-⊔⊔⊠⊠ ⊠□⊠◺□⊐◺ in◺□⊐ ⊏⊠⊠□◺◺. Give her a ⊏⊠⊐⊠□ ◺□⊠⊠◺□⊠ ⊠⊏762⊔. In return, she'll give you a ◺◺⊏◺ ⊠⊏ ◺⊐⊏◺□ ⊏◺⊠ found at the ◺⊠⊏ ⊠⊠⊐⊐□. Bring it back to ⊐ ⊔◺ ⊏⊠ and await further instructions.

35

PSA Challenge

DID YOU SOLVE IT?

Did you decode the message correctly? Let's find out. See if you can answer the questions correctly. Test your memory as well—don't peek!

1. What color basketball jersey was the penguin you needed to find wearing?

2. Where did you meet the penguin?

3. What did you give to her?

4. What did she give to you?

5. Who did you give the map to?

PENGUIN PUZZLE

Why is the letter *T* like an island?

⨅◻⌐⌐◻◔◖◻ ⌐◖◖ ⌐◖ ⌐⨉ ◖⌐⨅ ⨉⌐⌐⨉◻◻ ⨉⌐ ◖⌐◖◻⨉

Answers: 1. Red, 2. The Forest, 3. A flame thrower pizza, 4. A tuft of white fur, 5. G

36

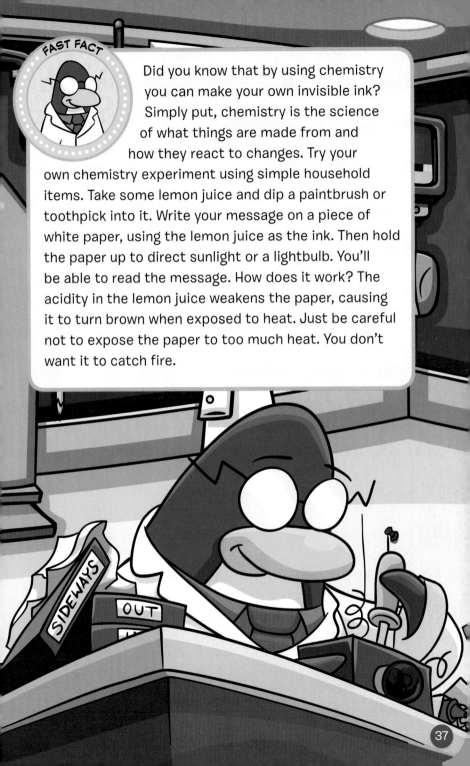

Did you know that by using chemistry you can make your own invisible ink? Simply put, chemistry is the science of what things are made from and how they react to changes. Try your own chemistry experiment using simple household items. Take some lemon juice and dip a paintbrush or toothpick into it. Write your message on a piece of white paper, using the lemon juice as the ink. Then hold the paper up to direct sunlight or a lightbulb. You'll be able to read the message. How does it work? The acidity in the lemon juice weakens the paper, causing it to turn brown when exposed to heat. Just be careful not to expose the paper to too much heat. You don't want it to catch fire.

SIDEWAYS

OUT

WANTED

HERBERT P. BEAR, ESQUIRE

PSA 00000001

WANTED FOR:

Breaking the Clock Tower

Possession of stolen blueprints and Clock Tower gear

Conspiracy to stop penguins from having fun

Holding a secret agent prisoner

Suspicion of causing an avalanche

Tampering with coins in the Gift Shop

Attempted theft of the boiler

Herbert P. Bear is considered dangerous and extremely grumpy.

WANTED

KLUTZY THE CRAB

PSA 00000002

WANTED FOR:

Aiding and abetting a known criminal

Escaping from HQ

Use caution when approaching Klutzy the Crab. He's got sharp claws.

PENGUIN PUZZLE

What are polar bears called when they get caught in the rain? ⊐⊠⌐◖◖⊠◖ ⊔◻⌐◖⊠◖

INTRODUCTION

Who is Herbert P. Bear and why is he out to destroy Club Penguin? From agents' accounts, we've been able to come up with the following information.

PROFILE

Name: Herbert P. Bear

Family: Unknown, but he spends most of his time with his accomplice, Klutzy the Crab.

Special characteristics: Herbert is a vegetarian, which means he does not eat meat, fish, or poultry.

Weaknesses: Herbert cannot swim, which is unusual for a polar bear. He also extremely dislikes being cold.

Greatest desire/motive: To live in a warm, sunny place with sandy beaches and fruit growing from the trees

Pet peeve: Cheerful penguins who love the cold

History: To escape the cold of the Arctic Circle, Herbert climbed on an iceberg and floated away from his home. After days at sea, he spotted an island in the distance and rowed toward it, thinking it was a tropical paradise. When Herbert realized the island was covered in snow, he tried to paddle away, but the iceberg tipped, dumping him into the ocean. Klutzy the Crab heard the bear's cries for help and pulled him to the shores of Club Penguin, a place even colder than the Arctic Circle.

Status: Herbert's whereabouts are unknown. We believe he is in hiding while he works out the details of his next devious plan. All agents are asked to be on alert and to check in frequently at HQ to see if they are needed to help stop Herbert once again.

FAST FACT

Though Klutzy's name might seem to imply otherwise, crabs are actually very good swimmers. Scientists tracked one that swam thirty-five miles in two days— a lot for a little crustacean. So I suppose it's not so surprising that when Herbert was stranded at sea, Klutzy was able to swim Herbert all the way to the Club Penguin shore.

PSA Challenge
FIND THE SECRET AGENT

A secret agent is waiting for you in the Plaza with a clue to help you solve a mission. The agent is in disguise. To find him, study each picture of the penguins in the Plaza carefully. Then read the clues to find which one is the agent.

(1)

(2)

(3)

(4)

(5)

(6)

1. The secret agent is carrying an item.
2. The secret agent is not wearing glasses.
3. The secret agent is wearing something on his head.
4. The secret agent's favorite color is green.
5. The secret agent is carrying sports gear.
6. The secret agent is wearing footwear.

Who is the secret agent? □⌐ ⌐⊓◙

Top Secret Missions

When the PSA has a case that needs investigating, it turns to its trusted agents to get the job done. If you feel you are ready to go on challenging missions, head over to HQ. To find out what assignments are available, click on the Top Secret Mission Ready computer file on the bottom-right of the screen. You could be called on to help a penguin in need or learn survival skills for your own training. You'll definitely have to help the PSA solve some strange acts of mischief that have occurred around the island. For each one you'll need to be brave and use your problem-solving skills.

Missions with a are locked until the required previous mission is completed. New missions are added from time to time so remember to keep checking HQ, especially if you see something unusual going on around the island. Sometimes the PSA will even put a coded message in *The Club Penguin Times*, so stay alert.

PENGUIN PUZZLE

Why do fish live in saltwater?

⬜◻◻⬜◻◻◻◻ ⬛◻⬛⬛◻⬛ ⬛◻⬛◻◻◻ ◻◻◻⬛ ◻⬛◻◻◻◻◻

Mission Success

Every mission takes skills to complete it. In fact, some of them can be rather difficult. But the PSA knows that secret agents are always up for a challenge. Here are a few tips the agency has compiled to help agents succeed:

- **Talk to everyone you see.** If you bump into a penguin on your journeys, make sure to stop and chat. You never know what you might find out. If that penguin needs help, give them a hand. Not only is it the secret agent way to be helpful, but you may get an extra reward in the end, too.
- **Pick up any objects you find.** Use your mouse to search new places and click to see if you can pick any objects up. Chances are if you can pick it up and put it in your inventory, it will come in handy later.
- **Use the tools in your spy phone.** Don't forget you've got some useful gadgets right in your spy phone. If something needs to be fixed or moved, try using one of these tools.
- **Try combining objects.** If you get stuck, try putting two items in your inventory together. It might create a new item that can help you in your mission.

- **Look for the secret code.** If you find anything written in the secret code, decipher it right away. It's sure to be of use to you.
- **Search high and low.** Use the map on the upper left of your screen to get around the island. Important places are often labeled. Make sure to check them out. Don't forget you can use your spy phone to get around quickly and easily.
- **Ask G.** If you get stuck, come back and speak with G. He might be able to help you out.
- **Don't give up.** If nothing seems to be working, go back to the last place you visited and look around to see if you missed anything.

In many missions there is also a small task you can do, or a mini mission. It's always a good idea to give them a try. Not only may it help in your main mission, but many of them involve helping a penguin in distress. And that's what being a good agent is all about!

Don't worry. You won't have to go into these missions unprepared. The following are the PSA's top secret, most classified mission files. Read them carefully. They contain hints to help you succeed.

Case of the Missing Puffles

Difficulty level:

Aunt Arctic, the beloved advice columnist and editor in chief of *The Club Penguin Times*, lost two of her pet puffles while on assignment. She is very upset and needs your help to locate her missing pets. Your assignment is to find the puffles and return them to Aunt Arctic.

Remember, some puffles can fly with the help of a propeller hat. So when you are searching high and low for Aunt Arctic's pets, you might want to focus your efforts up high.

If you complete this mission successfully, you'll receive the Golden Puffles Medal and a letter of thanks from Aunt Arctic.

Mission Hints

Hint #1:
Look for the answer to G's question in the
⊠□ⓘ ⓘ⊓⊠⊠.

Hint #2:
Use the ⊠⊠□⊠∟⊓ from your ⓘ⊠ⓗ ⊠⊓⊠⊠□
to fix the telescope.

Hint #3:
The ⊠⊠⊠□ will help you climb up the
⊠⊠ⓘ⊠ⓘ⊿⊓⊠.

G's Secret Mission

Difficulty level:

G needs you to test-drive a prototype of a new sled. The bad news is that the design of the sled still needs some work. The good news is that you get to test your survival skills when you crash-land in the Club Penguin wilderness.

Finding shelter and food, boiling water, and starting a fire are just some of the survival skills you'll need to succeed at this mission. Being alone in the woods might be a little spooky, but if you keep your wits about you and put to good use any items you might find, you'll be warm and cozy in no time.

If you complete this mission successfully, you will receive the Wilderness Survival Medal and a special message from G.

Mission Hints

Hint #1:

To answer G's riddle, head over to the ◙⊠Γ ⊓Γ⊠⊠ .

Hint #2:

Make a fishing pole by combining a ◙⊠Γ with a piece of ⊠⊠⊠⊓ .

Hint #3:

Look in the ◙⊠⊓⊓◙ for a ⊠⊠◙ to ⊔⊠Γ⊠ ◙⌐◙⊓⊠ in.

MISSION 3:

Case of the Missing Coins

Difficulty level: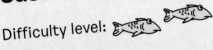

The coins from the Gift Shop have mysteriously gone missing. Your assignment is to locate the missing coins. If you're up to the challenge, you can also help fix a power outage at the Night Club.

The real challenge won't be to find the coins. It's getting them down that's the problem.

If you complete both missions successfully, you will receive the Electromagnet Award and a letter of thanks from a penguin you helped along the way.

Mission Hints

Hint #1:
Make sure to search under the ⊡⊠⊏⅃ in the manager's office. You'll find some valuable clues there.

Hint #2:
Use your ⊡⊠⊏⊠⌊⊓ to open the ⊠⊠⊡⊏⊠ ⌊⊠⊙.

Hint #3:
A ⊠⌐⊠⊏⊠ ⌊⊠⌐⊠ can be just the thing to deactivate a ⊠⌐⊓⊠⊏⊙.

Avalanche Rescue

Difficulty level:

There has been an avalanche on the Ski Hill. Four penguins are trapped on a cliff and in need of rescue. This won't be an easy task—the penguins are hard to reach.

You'll need to collect a lot of items to assist you in this rescue operation. Bring your best puzzle-solving skills to this mission because you'll need to navigate a tricky maze. You'll also want to take a closer look at what might have caused this avalanche. Look for clues on the mountaintop and near the Ski Lift.

If you complete this mission, you'll receive the Golden Sled Medal. If you finish the bonus mission as well, you'll get the Handy Penguin Award.

Mission Hints

Hint #1:

Look for the ⊔⊠⊠◘⊠ ⊔□⊠◙ in the Sport Shop.
You can use it to fix the ◙⊠⌐ ⊠⌐⊏◙.

Hint #2:

Take the ◙□⊠□◙∟⊠⊠◙ from the Lighthouse
to ⌐⊔⊠◙'◙ ⊠⊏⊏⌐∟□ in the Sport Shop.
Try looking through the ◙⌐⊠⌐⊠◙ with it.

Hint #3:

Combine the ⊠⌐⊏□ ⊠⊠□◙□⊠◙⊠ with the
⊏⌐◙⊓⌐⊠⌐ ⊠⊠⊠◙ and a piece of rope to
rescue the penguins.

Secret of the Fur

Difficulty level:

In previous missions, you will have discovered a strange piece of white fur and given it to G to analyze. Unfortunately the fur sample has been contaminated. Some strange substances have been detected on it. You'll need to collect larger amounts of these items and bring them back to G so he can determine exactly what—or who—the fur is from.

Be careful. Some penguins will tell you they spotted a monster on the island. You might need to come up with a clever way to trap it.

If you complete this mission, you'll receive the Golden Investigative Medal. If you finish the additional task in this mission, you'll get a thank-you pizza.

PIZZA

Mission Hints

Hint #1:
The ⌞⌧⌧⌟ from your ⌟⌧⌟ ⌧⌝⌧⌧⌟ can help fix the Furensic Analyzer 3000.

Hint #2:
Help the penguins in the ⌧⌝⌟⌟⌟ ⌧⌟⌧⌧⌧⌧ and the ⌞⌧⌐⌐⌟⌟ ⌟⌝⌧⌧ to find some of the items G needs.

Hint #3:
A ⌧⌟⌟ and a ⌧⌧⌧⌟ can make a good ⌟⌧⌟⌧. Try using a ⌞⌟⌧⌝⌧⌟ as bait.

MISSION 6:

Questions for a Crab

Difficulty level:

Finally! You've caught one of the suspects responsible for all the strange things that have been happening on the island. G is planning on asking the crab some questions, but it escapes from HQ before he can get started. Follow that crab and see where it leads you. But be careful. The crab has a large and cranky friend.

You'll return to a familiar spot in this mission: the wilderness where you crash-landed in G's secret mission. Use your previous experiences in this area to help you. In this mission you'll meet Herbert P. Bear, the polar bear who has been responsible for the strange happenings on the island. You'll also discover that the crab, named Klutzy, is Herbert's accomplice.

If you complete this mission, you will receive the Golden Box Medal and if you find an item that G has been looking for, you'll also get a copy of blueprints to the Electromagnet 1000.

Mission Hints

Hint #1:

Use the ⌐⌐⌐⌐⌐⌐⌐⌐ from your ⌐⌐⌐ ⌐⌐⌐⌐⌐ to get the ⌐⌐⌐⌐⌐⌐-⌐ ⌐⌐⌐⌐⌐⌐⌐ down from the tree.

Hint #2:

You'll need to find a way to melt snow. Heat things up by feeding the ⌐⌐⌐⌐⌐ ⌐⌐⌐⌐⌐-⌐ ⌐⌐⌐⌐⌐⌐⌐ sprinkled with ⌐⌐⌐ ⌐⌐⌐⌐.

Hint #3:

Before you leave Herbert's cave, make sure to grab the ⌐⌐⌐⌐⌐⌐, the ⌐⌐⌐⌐⌐⌐⌐⌐⌐⌐, and the ⌐⌐⌐⌐.

Clockwork Repairs

Difficulty level: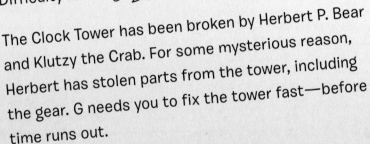

The Clock Tower has been broken by Herbert P. Bear and Klutzy the Crab. For some mysterious reason, Herbert has stolen parts from the tower, including the gear. G needs you to fix the tower fast—before time runs out.

This mission will test all of your secret agent skills. Make sure to speak to every penguin you encounter. You'll find out information that's crucial in helping to complete this task.

If you complete this mission, you'll receive the Silver Watch Medal. You'll also receive a blue jersey if the Blue Team decides to make you an honorary member.

Mission Hints

Hint #1:

Go to ▢▢▢ ▢▢▢▢ and ask the ▢▢▢▢ ▢▢▢▢ for the ▢▢▢▢▢▢.

Hint #2:

You'll need the ▢▢▢▢▢▢ on the middle shelf of the ▢▢▢▢▢▢▢▢ ▢▢▢▢▢▢. Unlock it by using the ▢▢▢.

Hint #3:

Grab a ▢▢▢▢▢▢ from ▢▢▢ ▢▢▢▢▢ and fill it with ▢▢▢▢. Give it to the ▢▢▢▢▢ ▢▢▢▢▢▢ along with the picture of the ▢▢▢▢. You'll need to play the ▢▢▢▢▢ for the puffle at ▢▢▢ ▢▢▢▢▢.

Mysterious Tremors

Difficulty level:

Mysterious earthquakes have been reported all over the island. G believes the cause is not natural. In fact, he thinks Herbert P. Bear is responsible. Track down Herbert and put a stop to his latest plan.

Herbert has made a drill and now he's digging underground tunnels around the island, causing the tremors. The key to finding Herbert will be repairing the Gift Shop, which was damaged in the tremors. So put your thinking cap on and get going.

If you complete this mission, you'll receive the Boiler-Spoiler Foiler Medal and if you locate an item stolen in a previous mission you'll get a cool gift from G.

Mission Hints

Hint #1:

Get a ⌧⌐◫◫⌟ for the penguin waiting in line in exchange for a piece of the ⌧⌟⌧.

Hint #2:

To get the other half of the ⌧⌟⌧, take the ⌐◻⌟⌧⌧⌟ ⌧⌧⌧⌧◻⌧⌧◻⌧ hat from HQ and give it to the ⌧◸◻◻⌧◻ in town along with a ⌞⌧⌧⌧⌐◻.

Hint #3:

To give the Gift Shop a lift, try either a ◻⌟⌧⌧◻⌧ ⌧◻ ⌞⌧◻⌟⌧ ◸⌧⌟⌟ or a ◻⌟⌧⌧⌧⌧⌧.

Spy and Seek

Difficulty level:

Herbert P. Bear's plans are becoming bolder and more dangerous and yet he still has managed to avoid capture. You are needed to gather intelligence on Herbert's whereabouts so the PSA can come up with a plan to apprehend him.

G will provide you with three tracking devices. You'll need to place them around the island: one as high as possible, one as low as possible, and one at sea. If you want to bear down on his location, you'll need to put all your previous on-the-job gadget expertise to work.

If you complete this mission, you'll receive a Medal of Excellence. If you help out some penguins playing *Find Four* in the Ski Lodge, you'll also get a box of chocolates.

Stealthy Spy Surveillance Medal •
For covert camera coverage and considerable cunning.

Thank you!

Chocolate: The Game

ission Hints

nt #1:
nd some ⬜◻⬜⬜⊠◻ ⌐◻⊠ in the ⊠⊠⌐◻⌐
o patch up the rubber duck. Then head over to
he ⌐⊠⌐⊠ to inflate it.

int #2:
ook in the ⊠⊠⌐⌐◻ ⌐◻◻⌐⌐ for a piece of string.
Go to the ⌐⊠⊠◻◻◻ and pick up some ◻◻⌐⌐⊠◻.
Combine these items with the ⬜⊠◻◻⊠⊠⌐⊠◻◻ G
gave you to make a ⊠⌐◻◻.

Hint #3:
Help the penguin at the ⊠⌐⊠◻ ◻⌐⌐⌐⊠ to place the
final transmitter. You'll need to click and drag the
◻⊠⊠⌐◻⊠ ⬜⊠⌐⊠⌐◻ to make the heavy metal beam
fall to the ⊠◻⌐◻.

MISSION 10:

Waddle Squad

Difficulty level:

An attempt is being made to catch Herbert P. Bear, using a golden puffle as bait. To do this, you'll need to work with two other secret agents. Your job in this mission is to make sure everything goes as planned. First, you need to make sure one agent has the fuel to get to a good lookout point. Then, you need to make sure the cage and Electromagnet 3000 are working correctly so you can trap Herbert when he comes looking for the golden puffle.

If you complete this mission successfully, you'll receive the Mission #10 Medal. And, if you help the penguin set up the special sale outside the Gift Shop, you can get the "Employee of the Month Award" as a bonus.

Mission Hints

Hint #1:

When you're helping ⬚⬚⬚ ⬚⬚⬚ Guy refuel, you'll need to go to the ⬚⬚⬚⬚⬚⬚⬚⬚ to get Cream Soda. Then, you must split the soda up evenly using three ⬚⬚⬚⬚⬚⬚. Look for a ⬚⬚⬚⬚⬚ with some hints in it so you can split the soda up evenly.

Hint #2:

To help Rookie set up the Electromagnet 3000, you need to find the ⬚⬚⬚⬚⬚ ⬚⬚⬚⬚ that is in the ⬚⬚. Be smart and get it the first time you're there, so you don't have to go back later.

Hint #3:

The ⬚⬚⬚⬚ that you are going to trap Herbert in is broken. Use the tools from your ⬚⬚⬚ ⬚⬚⬚⬚ to get into the ⬚⬚⬚⬚⬚⬚. Put the gears back where they belong to get the cage working!

Stay tuned for more exciting missions on clubpenguin.com!

Now It's Time to Organize Your Own Missions!

The fun doesn't stop once you've completed the missions. When you visit HQ you'll see other agents around. Why not get everyone together and come up with your own mission ideas? It's a great way to keep your skills sharp so you are ready for the next new mission. Below are a few suggestions, but you can also use your imagination.

Penguin Patrol

Since a big part of an agent's job is keeping the island safe, gather your agent buddies and decide where you should patrol. You can all wear your secret agent clothing, or you could dress to blend in. Grab any instruments you might have and go undercover as a band and play on the stages at the Pizza Parlor or the Lighthouse, or even in the orchestra at The Stage. While you are playing, you should keep an eye out for any signs of trouble.

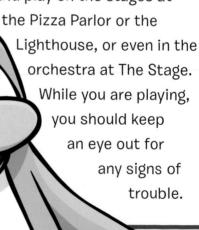

Here are a few other undercover ideas: Everyone could go incognito, acting like they're simply walking their puffles through the Plaza, or put on their bathing suits and hit the Beach, the Dock, or the Cove to patrol these areas unnoticed. Go undercover as waiters, chefs, and cashiers to foil any attempted thefts at the Pizza Parlor. The possibilities are endless!

Penguin Pals

New penguins arrive on the shores of Club Penguin every day. Some of them feel a little lost and confused at first. You and your fellow secret agents can help them dive right into the fun.

Get together a team of agents to look for any newcomers. Offer to show them around, or answer any questions they might have. Not only will you be giving them a cool first experience on Club Penguin, but you might make a new buddy, too.

PENGUIN PUZZLE

It is the part of the bird that is not in the sky.
It can swim in the ocean and yet remain dry.
What is it? ⅃ ₒ∩⅃⊐⊠ₒ

Secret Agent Meetings

Agents have a lot to talk about. So why not hold a secret agent meeting at HQ? Chat about your experiences as agents, share mission hints, and plan missions of your own.

Mission Maker

Gather up your agent buddies and assign missions. Take turns sending groups of agents out on a special assignment. Get creative! You can send agents to patrol the Ski Hill, provide security for the Gift Shop, or search for polar bear tracks by the Snow Forts.

Pin Pursuit

You've just read in *The Club Penguin Times* that a new pin has been hidden. Who would be better at finding it than a group of agents? Head over to HQ and organize a search.

Hide-and-Seek

Turn this well-known game into a test of your tracking and camouflage skills. While you are at HQ, divide the agents into two teams. Everyone can even wear team colors to make it easier to recognize hiding team members. One team is "It." The other team will hide first in an agreed-upon location, such as Town Center. Before you start, decide on an emote that will be used when a hidden player is found. The winking smiley face is a good choice for this. The "It" team counts to ten and then the chase is on. When you find an agent, walk up to them and use the emote. That player then has to return to HQ. Once all the players on a team have been found, switch and let the "It" players hide.

Do you know there are a few places on Club Penguin where you can hide and see other penguins but they won't know you are there? Head over to the Pizza Parlor and walk over to the pizza oven. There are sacks of flour stacked up in the corner on the floor. Stand behind them and no one will be able to see you. You can also become invisible in the Mine Shack, if you stand behind the icy stalagmite on the lower-right of the screen. Search for other good hiding spots like this—they're everywhere!

PSA Challenge
AGENT ANAGRAMS

Put your puzzle-solving skills to the test with these tricky anagrams. An anagram is what you get when you take one word and rearrange the letters to form one or more new words from it. For example, if you take the letters in snowball, you can make lawn slob or wall snob.

Here are twelve anagrams made from the names of penguins, places, and things on Club Penguin. Rearrange the letters in the words to spell out one of the words in the word bank.

WORD BANK

Aunt Arctic

Bean Counters

Cart Surfer

Forest

Gary

Jet pack

Mine Shack

Penguins

Pet Shop

Secret agents

Snow

The Stage

1. Softer
2. Pine sung
3. Gas teeth
4. Curtain cat
5. Beacon unrest
6. Step hop
7. Stage centers
8. Gray
9. Crater furs
10. Mice shank
11. Owns
12. Jack pet

How to Maintain a Secret Identity

It can be difficult keeping your secret agent status a secret. For instance, remember when earthquakes shook up the island? Penguins who were not agents had no idea that the tremors were caused by Herbert P. Bear. As an agent, you might want to discuss this exciting news with all your buddies, whether they are agents or not. But then being a secret agent wouldn't be very secret, would it?

The best way of maintaining a secret identity is by not telling anyone. It seems simple but it's easy to slip up. For instance, if a penguin asks you, "Are you an agent?" your first instinct, like all good agents, would be to answer honestly. But that would give your secret away. You could always say, "That's classified information," or, "Secret agents are sworn to secrecy, so if I was an agent, I wouldn't be able to tell you."

If you have to talk about being a secret agent with another secret agent buddy, go to HQ. You'll find lots of your fellow agents there and you can chat all about the PSA and its secrets.

There is a problem at the Night Club. Your help is needed. Use your detective skills and knowledge of Club Penguin to solve the Case of the Pet Puffle. The Night Club, with its brightly lit dance floor and upbeat music, is usually a happy place. But instead of cheerful penguins dancing on the floor, a pink penguin and a red penguin are arguing about who owns a purple puffle.

"My purple puffle loves to dance. We come here every day and hit the floor. We were dancing together when this penguin came over and said it was his puffle," the pink penguin said.

"My puffle doesn't like dancing," the red penguin said. "It loves playing on its trampoline. Then we go to the Pizza Parlor and pig out on an extra-large spicy squid pizza."

What do you think? Who does the purple puffle belong to: the pink penguin or the red penguin? Turn the page for the answer.

You heard all you needed to crack the case.
The purple puffle belongs to the pink penguin.

It's a fact that purple puffles love to dance and are very picky eaters. So when the red penguin said that the purple puffle's favorite thing to do was eat pizza and jump on a trampoline, you knew he wasn't telling the truth. The red penguin apologized to the pink penguin and admitted he made up the story because he thought the purple puffle was cute and wanted one of his own. You took the red penguin to the Pet Shop and helped him pick out a puffle of his own for a pet. Pink puffles love both jumping rope and the trampoline and aren't fussy about what they eat. In the end, everyone was happy and once again you helped keep Club Penguin a fun and safe place.

PENGUIN PUZZLE

What does not burn in a fire and does not drown in water? ⌐∟□

Since penguins enjoy playing on the Iceberg so much, I decided to do a little investigating and find out exactly what causes icebergs to form. I discovered that icebergs are blocks of ice that break off from the edge of a glacier. Glaciers are huge bodies of ice and snow that build up over thousands of years. Icebergs are composed of freshwater, so the ice is safe to use as ice cubes or to be melted down to drink. Maybe that's why all those penguins are always drilling out on the Iceberg.

PENGUIN PUZZLE

Why did the penguin cross the ocean?

PSA Challenge
THE FINAL MISSION

To see how much your agent skills have improved, this final challenge will test all the skills you've learned in this book. Good luck.

1. What was the name of the play that asked this question: "To fish or not to fish"?
   ☐☐☐ ☐☐☐☒☐☐ ☐☐☐☐

2. Unscramble this word to find the name of a place on Club Penguin.
   Thread square ☐☐☐☐☒☐☐☒☐☐☒☐

3. Find the number of tables in the Pizza Parlor, the number of sofas on the first floor of the Coffee Shop, the number of lifeguard chairs at both the Cove and the Underground Pool, and the number of rocking horses in the Ski Lodge. Add them all together. What number do you get? ☐☐☐☐☐

4. It lives without a body, speaks without a mouth, hears without ears, and is born in the air. What is it? ☐☐☐☒

5. When does a secret agent reveal their identity to penguins who aren't agents? ☒□◙□☒ !

6. Herbert is at it again! He's stolen a set of G's blueprints. An agent overheard him saying he's hidden them in a secret place in the mountains that many penguins don't know about. Where are the blueprints hidden? ⊐☒☒☒

Now take the first letter of each answer to spell out a message. Do you know what it is? ◙□□ □☒⊐

Keep Up the Good Work

Congratulations! You've done an excellent job on all the challenges you've encountered in this handbook.

Remember to always be vigilant and keep an eye out for any mysterious happenings on the island. Check back to HQ often to see if you are needed for a new mission. Be alert when reading *The Club Penguin Times*. You can sometimes find coded messages for agents only hidden in its pages.

Keep this handbook safe. The PSA has trusted us with highly classified information. We wouldn't want it to fall into the flippers of a penguin who is not an agent, or worse, the paws of Herbert P. Bear!

FINAL FACT

On behalf of the PSA, thank you for all the hard work you've done to make Club Penguin a safe place. I'm looking forward to working on missions with you in the future. Until then, ⊏⊐⊠□◎□⊠⊠ .